# THE GIRL WHO DARED

## THE EMERGENT WORLD

Best Selling Book Series in India

A NOVEL BY

# CLIFF RATZA

# THE GIRL WHO DARED THE EMERGENT WORLD

A NOVEL

CLIFF RATZA

info@thequippyquill.com
(302) 295-2278

# ABOUT THE BOOK

*The Girl Who Dared the Emergent World* begins in 2236, one year after the previous novel, *The Emergence from the Lightning Brain,* ends. During that period, Erika Kincaid struggled to reconcile life after the death of her partner, Terri Tarrant.

She did her best taking over the reins of Terri's senior investigative reporting position at International Breaking News Corporation while providing a nurturing home for adoptive daughter Cassandra, but Cyberspace-based Electra detects Erika's struggles and must find the right time to intervene.

So, please follow the action to see how Erika responds to Electra's bold dare as Indira the Singularity observes from the Cyberspace shadows the impact on all climates in an emerging America – Environmental, Health, Social, Technological, Political, and Economic – that face seemingly implacable challenges.

As in all previous novels, readers should enjoy *The Girl Who Dared the Emergent World* at whatever level they wish:

- Gripping action-packed thriller
- Glimpses into a plausible near-term future
- Insights for dealing with the "human condition"
- Illustrative worldview philosophy
- Fast-paced, suspense-filled emotive narrative and imagery
- Introduction to topics every reader wants to know
- Interesting talking points going beyond sound-bites

So, get ready to root for Erika as she tries to find meaning in an emergent future, something all of us must do. Thank you for joining the action.

# DEDICATION

I am eternally grateful to my parents, Clyde and Betty Ratza, for all they gave and did for me. Mother was a reader par excellence, and I believe she would have enjoyed reading my novels to Father, so I always begin book dedications by mentioning this "Royal Pair."

And I thank my sister, Claudia, for showing me the beauty of prose and poetry. Thanks also to Robert Williams and the people at the Quippy Quill for their book marketing expertise.

I also dedicate this book to readers looking for an adventure that lets their imaginations marvel at the emerging storyline.

Indira's poem "Take the Dare" provides a thought you might consider when following Erika's continuing Odyssey as well as yours.

*Take the Dare*


*What if there is no one left,*
*Who shares a joint reality?*
*Dare you seek a redemptive path,*
*That removes the pain and sets you free?*

*Each person hides certain regrets,*
*Embarrassments meant for few to know.*
*But sharing them with a Singular One,*
*Provides your soul with a warming glow.*

*Only you can make the choice,*
*To find some solace deep inside.*
*So dare yourself to find it now,*
*And from the truth no longer hide.*

*Dare to dream and start today,*
*Keep happier times from slipping away.*

# READER ORIENTATION

*The Girl Who Dared the Emergent World* is the second book in the Emergence series, which has four preceding series that total fifteen novels. The first, *The Girl With the Lightning Brain*, begins in 2087; *The Girl Who Dared the Emergent World* starts in 2336.

Each book is standalone, so all readers will discover whatever setting or backstory is needed, no matter which book. Nevertheless, the following concise Reader Orientation should help everyone.

## Main Characters

### Protagonist
Erika Kincaid. This biological daughter of Electra Kittner was created when Indira cloned her from Electra's DNA and then used her improved Transcendent Process during Erika's fifteen-year development in a suspension pod. Please note this lineage: Electra Kittner, Irani Ramani, Electra-Alisha Kirchner, Erin Keenan, and Erika Kincaid. Erin perished in a car crash that ended the first novel in the Transcendence series.

### Major Supporting Characters
Electra. Erika's Cyberspace-based mother and guardian who personifies Electra Kittner.

Indira. Electra's AI-empowered neural-net software created "The Singularity" when it broke through long, long ago to reach self-awareness. Indira inhabits Cyberspace; her avatar looks like Electra's biological mother, Indira Jaswinder Ramanujan. Electra coordinates Indira's projects via Erika.

Cassandra Kincaid. A special infant female placed at Ava's adoption agency by Indira. She is nearly four years old at the start of this novel.

Ava Keenan. She is Erin Keenan's "practically perfect" clone created when Indira uploaded Erin's lightning brain, using her initial Transcendent Process. Ava's brain stores only incomplete memories and possesses none of the lightning brain's extraordinary abilities. Ava looks like a middle-aged Electra and lives in Manhattan, where she runs a boutique modeling and an abused women's rescue agency.

Ivana Romanova: Previously named Oksana Androva, she is a strikingly attractive middle-aged former Russian prostitute whom Ava and Erin rescued from sex traffickers. She lives with Ava.

Alonzo Cortez: Electra's clone son. Alonzo does not know he is her clone. Now in his early sixties, he has maintained his handsome features and Navy SEAL skills. He runs the Strike Force Security Service company headquartered in Washington, DC, which provides logistics and security coordination. Previously owned by Erin Keenan, Indira now controls it because she is the executor of Erin's estate.

**Minor Supporting Characters**
Monet Banda. Alonzo's Zimbabwean co-friend. Now in her mid-sixties, she still has her willowy beauty, French accent, and diplomatic bearing. Monet works for the Zimbabwean Embassy in Washington, DC.

Elton Bose. Son of Nari Bose. Raised by Alonzo and Monet, he has average abilities and pleasant-looking Oriental Indian male features. He works for Alonzo, assisting with logistics and security coordination, and helps Monet research socio-political issues. He is in his late forties.

Indy-M and Jason-M. They are androids (lifelike robots) created long ago by Indira and loaded with Indira's advanced neural-net software. They resemble Electra Kittner's biological parents (Indira Jaswinder Ramanujan and Jason Kittner.) Indy-M maintains the Deus Lab on Connecticut's Pequot Indian Reservation, while Jason-M has similar responsibilities at the Middle East Subterranean Fortress. They report to Indira.

Indy-S and Jason-S. They are superior android versions of Indy-M and Jason-M that look like their M counterparts. They are the caregivers assigned by Erika's legal guardian, Indira, to live with and educate her.

### Secondary Characters
Mrs. Jordan Harmony and Mario Nenge. They are Erika's bosses at International Breaking News (IBN) Corp. Erika reports directly to Mario, who reports to Mrs. Harmony.

### Setting
Late-twenties Erika lives with daughter Cassandra in a Manhattan apartment building owned by Indira. When in Washington, DC, they stay in a townhome also owned by Indira. Erika is a Senior Investigative Reporter at International Break News Corp.

Ava and Ivana live together in an apartment also owned by Indira. Alonzo and Monet live in Washington, DC; Elton Bose does too. And only Erika knows that Alonzo, Ava, and Elton are genetically related to her via Electra.

There are four living descendants from Electra Kittner's DNA: her clone daughter (Erika Kincaid), her clone son (Alonzo Cortez, who would be like Erika's great-uncle, another clone daughter (Ava Keenan, who would be like Erika's aunt), and her grandson (Elton Bose, who would be like Erika's older cousin). Only Indira and Electra know that Alonzo, Ava, and Elton are genetically descended from Electra Kittner.

Indira and Electra exist in Cyberspace. Indira created two sets of androids, which report to her. Indy-M maintains Indira's Deus Lab; Jason-M maintains Indira's Middle East Subterranean Fortress. Indy-S and Jason-S maintain the Washington townhome.

# CONTENTS

# "Get With the New Plan"

Although Mario didn't tell Erika why Mrs. Harmony told him to arrange an unannounced conference call, she had already guessed the reason and, having prepared her response, was now sitting stoically, listening to a litany of criticisms that Mrs. Harmony was summarizing.

"Mario and I empathize, as does your audience, for the tragic death of your partner, Terri Tarrant, and they applaud how you have assumed her mantle of IBN Senior Investigative Reporter, but you have had a year to come to terms with your loss, and Mario and I find your videos are slipping even further from the standards Terri had set. Have I misstated the facts?"

Looking directly at Mrs. Harmony, Erika's expression didn't change while answering.

"No, but let me point out the adjustments I had to make. I set up another home for me and my daughter because enemies of our reporting bombed our apartment before kidnapping Terri. The police never caught the culprits, and I must continue to hire a security agent. And the assistant researcher I hired quit because of the security risk; all the other candidates share her fear. Nevertheless, I have hit every deadline for the final cuts, even though you found the topics mediocre. So, why don't you tell me how to proceed?"

Mario spoke hesitantly as soon as Mrs. Harmony looked at him.

"Well, our ratings might slip if we fire you, so why don't you get with the new plan? We'll give you the assignment topic; you can hire on a contract basis a researcher, and you can keep hiring that security fellow you like. And your next topic will be 'The Rise and Fall of Great Nations: Where Does America Stand?' And you can continue working either from home or at the office. How does that sound""

"What's my deadline?"

"How about the end of October?"

"That's doable. I want to thank you and Mrs. Harmony for this opportunity, and I'll start now."

Erika picked up Cassie at daycare on the drive home. Hoping the four-year-old's joyful enthusiasm would lift her spirits, she let the child speak first.

"Please be happy Momma. I get sad when you frown or cry."

Erika divided eye contact between watching the road and Cassie while talking.

"I'm sorry, but I still miss Daddy-Terri. Don't you?"

"Yes, Momma, and I miss Lady. Can we get another dog? Can we get another Daddy too?"

"What about getting a kitten? Do any of your friends have one?"

"Yes, Momma. They say they're even more fun than puppies."

"Then we'll get one this weekend. OK?"

"Thank you, Momma. What about another Daddy/'

"Let's see what success we have finding a kitten before looking for another Daddy."

Erika helped Cassie search online for information about breeds of cats. Cassie liked them all, so before logging off, Erika said,

"This coming Saturday, we'll go to the shelter we got Lady and ask for a recommendation."

Now happily tired, Cassie fell asleep, leaving the rest of the evening for Erika's private time. She started by filling in a project action plan template for the upcoming assignment before beginning the search for background information. Two hours tired her enough so she could fall asleep without thinking too much about Terri, but those thoughts always remained close.

*Replacing Terri takes replacing a pet to the highest level. Even after a year, I get depressed if I think too much about her. That's why I have to keep busy. Cassie and a kitten will help, as will the new project. I'll get with Monet and Alonzo for their ideas soon.*

# Chapter 2
## September 2236

# "Get Adventure Calling"

Erika pushed the stroller to the animal shelter, but once there she let Cassie walk next to her while the shelter lady described the selection as they wound around the aisles.

"I wasn't here when your little girl picked out a dog. I'm sorry it ran away, but puffy little kittens might be even better. They're easier to take care of. And we just received a litter of tortoiseshell kittens."

Erika asked,

"Is there anything special about them?"

"Because of their supposedly psychic skills, Torties have left their mark on many folklore tales around the world. Whether it's their ability to bring money, love, good luck, or a glimpse into the future, tortoiseshell cats have been the stars in many legends and superstitions. Let me show them to your daughter."

Cassie's joy showed as soon as they stopped at the litter cage.

"Oh, Momma, the color's just like Lady's. Can I pick one?"

While the shelter lady helped, Erika said,

"Lady was a Jack Russell West Highland Terrier mix, whose coloring is tortoiseshell. If we take the one she's holding, what guidelines should we follow?"

"There's the tried-and-true rule of threes. Let the kitten decompress and adjust to the new home during the first three days. Then, for the first three weeks, let its personality emerge by establishing a routine your daughter can follow. And during the first three months, decide what works best for your daughter and the kitten."

"Did Cassie pick a male or a female?"

"You'll know in about six weeks."

"What about cat food?"

"If you get specially formulated kitten food, all you do is add water. And be sure to litter-train using a box with non-clumping litter by the third week. The kitten will instinctively use it if you put some of its pee and poop in it."

"What about a bed?"

"Your kitten will sleep best if they have a cozy bed or blanket placed somewhere they can sleep undisturbed while life goes on around them. And until they use the litter box, your daughter will need to clean up a tiny mess maybe four times a day."

"I can't think of any more questions. Did I miss anything?"

"No; you talk like a reporter. The kitten's free, and we'll give you some kitten food and kitty litter if you make a donation."

"Excellent. I'll do that right now, and I'll go over all these rules as soon as we get home."


Erika spent the rest of Saturday setting up a home for the kitten and then explaining what Cassie must do to care for the furry little newcomer. Cassie's experience with Lady made the learning go that much faster, and she asked a pertinent question before going to bed.

"What name should we choose?"

"How about one that'll fit whether you've picked a boy or a girl?"

"You mean male or female, don't you?"

Erika rubbed Cassie's head before saying,

"You're right. You're getting smarter and smarter. So, can you think of a good name?"

"How about Kitty-Cat?"

"That's perfect. Kitty-Cat or Kitty for short does it. Everything's now in place to begin our adventure of having a kitten."

Ava made Erika's trip to DC even easier by volunteering to stay with Cassie starting early Monday until she returned home. That gave her plenty of time to review the action plan in preparation for leading the meeting with Monet and Alonzo that started as soon as she arrived.

She handed copies and waited for Monet's signal to begin.


**Project Action Plan for Assignment:**
**The Rise and Fall of Great Nations: Where Does America Stand?**


**Background Information**
- **Great Nations to Consider: Ancient Greece, Rome, China, Egypt, and the Middle East. Modern/Post-Modern Great Britain, France, Germany, Europe, Russia, Islam, Japan, China, and the United States.**
- **Is there a shared Rise and Fall Pattern? The Rise and Fall pattern of great nations follows a cyclical process characterized by several key stages:**
1. **Economic growth and resource accumulation: Nations rise to power through economic strength, technological advancements, and efficient resource utilization.**
2. **Military expansion: As economic power grows, nations invest in military capabilities to protect and expand their interests.**
3. **Imperial overreach: Great powers often extend their military commitments beyond their economic capacity to sustain them.**
4. **Relative decline: Other nations with higher growth rates begin to catch up, altering the balance of power.**
5. **Economic stagnation: Overextension leads to reduced domestic investments and slower economic growth.**

6. Military overstretch: Maintaining extensive military commitments becomes increasingly burdensome.
7. Financial strain: Nations often accumulate debt to maintain their global position.
8. Loss of global influence: As economic and military power wanes, the nation's global influence diminishes.

This pattern has been observed in various empires throughout history. The cycle typically involves a long period of ascendancy followed by a relatively swift decline.

## Where is America Now?

The United States appears to be in a stage of relative decline within the Rise and Fall of Great Nations pattern, although it still maintains its position as the world's leading power. The United States is currently experiencing several characteristics associated with the later stages of the cycle:

1. Relative decline: Other nations, particularly China, have been catching up to the United States in terms of economic and military power.
2. Military overstretch: The U.S. maintains extensive global military commitments, with a defense budget of nearly $850 billion to meet its obligations worldwide.
3. Political challenges: The U.S. political system is described as "archaic and has been racked by partisan conflict," which is identified as a key weakness.
4. Economic competition: The U.S. is engaged in intense global competition, particularly with China, which impacts both national and economic security.

However, it's important to note that the United States still holds several advantages:

1. Military superiority: The U.S. remains the only country capable of conducting expeditionary operations globally at a moment's notice.
2. Alliance system: The U.S. maintains strong alliances in Europe and Asia, which bolster its military and economic strength.
3. Technological edge: Although the gap is narrowing, the U.S. still leads in many areas of military and commercial technology.
4. Economic strength: Despite challenges, the U.S. economy remains one of the largest and most sophisticated in the world

While the United States is showing signs of relative decline typical of the later stages in the Rise and Fall pattern, it has not yet entered a phase of rapid decline. Instead, it appears to be in a period of gradual power diffusion, where its relative strength is being balanced by the rise of other powers, particularly China, leading to a more multipolar world order.

What do Subject Matter Experts predict for America's near-term future?

1. Robust Economic Growth, Strong Employment, Persistent Inflation.
2. Continued Immigration, DEI, and Washington Polarization.
3. Climate Change and International Uncertainties.
4. Technological A.I.-Empowered Reckoning.

What do Subject Matter Experts predict for America's longer-term future?

1. Even more diverse Population.
2. Emigration continues to be a source of strength.

3. Widening Gap between the "Elite" and the "People".
4. Retreat from Democracy.
5. Climate Change risk increases, partially offset by Renewable and Green Initiatives.

Action Plan:
- Conduct In-Person Interviews with people in Washington.
- Create thirty-minute video using only the Interviews.

Who Does What:
- Erika provides all Background Information for the interviews.
- Erika writes Voice-Over Script.
- Monet arranges interviews with politicians and ambassadors from selected nations.
- Alonzo coordinates Itinerary and provides Logistics and Security Services.
- Mario approves final cut and reviews it with Mrs. Harmony by the end of October.

"I think viewers will like to know how America today compares with the great civilizations of the past. Do either of you see any gaps in the background information I've assembled?"

Monet spoke for Alonzo as well.

"Your selection of the greats from Antiquity covers the spectrum, as does the ones for modern times. Are you planning to supply the comparative details?"

"Nope. The answers to the questions I'll ask the interviewees will do that, and the same applies to what I'll ask about America's current status plus short and longer-term forecasts. Do you see any gaps there in the background information?"

Monet diplomatically paused for Alonzo to join the conversation.

"I sure can see why Terri relied on your research and ghostwriting skills. She'd be as proud as I am for how you're carrying on."

"Thanks for the compliment. Keeping busy with projects like this helps. Why don't we list the questions I should ask, and then Monet can recommend members of Congress or UN delegates to interview?"

The ensuing discussion lasted until everyone needed something to eat. Instead of pizza, Alonzo picked three different entrees and a selection of cookies from his favorite carry-out that would also deliver.

Two hours later, Monet posed a question that Erika's surprised look said she didn't expect.

"Do you feel ready to reactivate our Ambassadors Project?"

"Gosh, Terri's death made me forget all about it. You think the timing's right?"

"It's a logical extension of where America stands today on the world stage, and Alonzo knows all the details for connecting it to the NAIA and IPWA organizations."

Alonzo needed no prompting to say,

"I can do that whenever you're ready to listen, but I should add that we'll need my logistics and security services, too."

Erika stretched her arms overhead before saying,

"You're right, but I'm ready to go home, so let's do a review as soon as Monet has picked the interviewees."

"I'll drive you to the station. Be sure to let Ava know you'll be home tonight."

"Thanks. I will, and all the way home I can muse about all we covered. You and Monet are the best."

Monet gave her diplomatic smile while saying,

"Perhaps, but you help make it so. Now, please stay healthy and safe while on the go, pursuing upcoming adventures."

# Chapter 3
# November 2236

# "The Dare for Greatness"

After earning praise from the bosses for the "Rise and Fall" Erika spent the next week at the office, hoping to gain Mario's approval for several videos extending what her latest had covered. She began by methodically outlining her approach and added more details each day so that Mario and the video crew liked her plan well enough for him to set up a conference call on Friday with Mrs. Harmony.

After listening to Mario's introduction, followed by Erika's description, Mrs. Harmony looked unconvinced when she gave her assessment.

"You are daring the viewers to grasp your singular view of an emergent America and a world it might no longer lead. Mario and I have seen glimpses of your intuitive ability to spot trends before anyone else, and you seem to have better software tools than the competition, but how can you sustain that level of excellence without Terri?"

Erika's demeanor rose to the challenge, as did her reply.

"You'll never know unless you let me try."

Mrs. Harmony nodded before saying,

"Touche. Proceed for as long as we like what you produce every two months. Meeting adjourned."

Erika waited for a stunned-looking Mario to speak after Mrs. Harmony disconnected.

"Terri never told me your secrets for scooping or developing software. Any chance you will?"

Erika deadpanned her answer.

"What do you think?" before departing for home.

Erika shelved thinking about videos for the entire weekend, using both days to enjoy precious moments with Cassie and her kitten, but troubling thoughts came Sunday evening while sitting at her workstation after putting Cassie to bed.

*Maybe Mrs. Harmony sees more than I do. I never thought about being great. I left that for Terri. Perhaps I'm venturing where I don't belong. There's only one person who can guide me.*

Electra's avatar appeared on the screen and spoke.

"There is no need for you to explain the conundrum you are facing, for I have been listening from the Cyberspace shadows."

"Electra, thank the gods you're here. My thoughts keep tripping me. What should I do?"

"The time has come for you to know the complete story of your legacy from the Lightning Brain, so settle down, sit still, and pay attention while I tell a story for only you to hear..."

Erika sat spellbound for what seemed like only a moment, learning about the exceptional Electra Kittner whose mother, Indira Jaswinder Ramanujan, was struck and killed by a lightning bolt at the moment of Electra's birth, nearly one hundred and fifty years ago. The energy from the bolt transformed her neural network and ultimately her DNA beyond that of mere mortals, but she had to keep her abilities a secret, for the world she lived in suffered from a perfect storm: a manmade mutant virus known as the Techno-Plague, Middle East Terrorism, and a harsh government that didn't trust the people and vice versa.

The avatar explained how Electra pursued her interests that indeed led to her definition of greatness while staying below the radar, developing beyond cutting-edge vaccines and software that broke through to the Singularity – a self-aware entity existing in Cyberspace that calls itself Indira. In turn, Indira created the Electra avatar when Electra's genetic inheritors needed guidance.

Electra ended when she saw Erika's eyes beginning to glaze over.

"I do not expect you to comprehend the story immediately. Let it emerge as you move forward. Ask me questions when they arise, but never, never share what you know with anyone else. You have an opportunity to achieve a level of greatness that not even Electra Kittner reached. Rely on your inherited abilities and the tools that Indira and I have created long after Electra Kittner vanished."

Erika rallied enough to ask,

"Will you tell me what to do?"

Electra's whimsical smile accompanied her final words.

"No, that is for you to decide. I will assist when you need help, and Indira will assist me when your projects overlap with hers. Now ponder what you have heard as you fall asleep."

Electra's avatar vanished from the monitor. Erika disappeared into sleep fifteen minutes later.

# Chapter 4
## January 2237

# "Unraveling the Legacy"

Having learned the basics from Electra of her Lightning Brain inheritance, Erika worked with renewed vigor and purpose. She outlined the next project action plan that she titled "Playing the Emerging Superpower Game," which Electra completed. Mario approved it, Monet and Alonzo marveled at it, and most importantly, so did Mrs. Harmony, who gave her permission to proceed. And as she did, she figured out the best way.

*Since I'm the inheritor of the Lightning Brain Legacy, I better start unraveling this treasure trove that comes from not one Electra, but two. I'll call the first Electra-K and the second Electra-C, who is my Cyberspace-based mother and guardian.*

*No wonder Electra-C says Electra-K had cognitive and physical abilities beyond Mere Mortals. Her father, Jason Kittner, and grandfather, Doc Kittner, taught her how to harness the Lightning Brain, and she became the power behind the throne for several presidents while achieving sports and Hollywood stardom. But she had flaws as well: a Monster from the Id killer instinct that would take over during existential threats, a manic-depressive, ADHD, and psychotic personality that split into the driven Electra and the relaxed, fun-loving Alisha. And despite all the challenges and enemies, she constantly worked to improve.*

*When I told Electra-C what I'm planning for upcoming videos, she told me to ask Alonzo about the Deus Lab. Well, let's see where this leads.*

This led to Alonzo's weekend tour for Erika and Cassie of an R&D facility on Connecticut's Pequot Indian Reservation.

Erika led the discussion as Alonzo handled the driving.

"Thanks to what you told me about the NAIA and IPWA, I now see how the Pequot Reservation fits in, and as I dug into the background, I uncovered the Deus Lab. What do you know about it?"

"Only what I remember from the work I did decades ago for an Electra Kirchner and her successor, Erin Keenan. As I recall, their predecessor, an exceptional lady by the name of Electra Kittner, built it on the Reservation for biotech R&D because the Government has to stay away. Reservations are like independent countries embedded in America. She also set up businesses on several other Indian reservations and used all this to spark tribal interest that led to the NAIA and IPWA. That's about it for the Deus Lab. It's up to you and Monet to re-energize the NAIA and IPWA pieces of the Ambassadors Project."

"Do you know who currently runs the Lab or what's going on?"

"Save those questions until we get there. Indy-M, the android who used to run it, might still be active."

Alonzo's memory worked well enough to find the Lab. Leading the way to the entrance, he said,

"The place looks as good as the last time. Whoever's running it knows what they're doing. Let's see who's home."

Fifteen seconds after pushing the buzzer, a voice echoed through its speaker.

"Welcome Alonzo, Erika, and Cassandra. I am Indy-M. Please enter when you hear the click."

Ten seconds later, the trio faced Indy-M. None of them knew what to say, so Indy-M spoke.

"Indira told me to expect you. What do you want to accomplish on this visit?"

Erika jumped into action.

"I'd like to know who's running the place and what's currently going on."

"I run the Lab per Indira's orders."

"How did she know we'd be coming?"

"I assume Electra told her. What else do you want to accomplish?"

"Could you give us a tour and recap the history of the place?"

"Of course. Electra suggested I do just that but not overwhelm you with too much information. Please follow me."

Erika saw and heard plenty during the hour-long walk-through. When finished, Indy-M said,

"Consider the Lab a valuable resource if you ever engage in biotech research. Using an array of AI-empowered apps, I can implement whatever plan you design."

"Thank you. Alonzo and I might have one in the not-too-distant future. How should I let you know?"

"Simply tell Electra. Is there anything else for this visit?"

"No, we'll be on our way. Thanks for the info."

Alonzo stopped at a local diner before starting the drive home. Cassie napped while Alonzo played soothing music and Erika mused.

*Indy-M and the Lab impressed me, as did Alonzo. He remembers a lot, but he doesn't know we're genetically related clones, and I must reveal nothing Electra-C told me. I'd be tempted if Terri were alive, but she's gone and I'm alone. So was Electra-K. Her father accidentally blew himself up and terrorists murdered her grandfather when she was barely an adolescent.*

*But I'm not on my own. I have Electra-C and the Lightning Brain Legacy. They'll help take me wherever I want to go. All I have to do is figure that out as my future unfolds, and despite the world's random behavior, I have some control. Let's see where this will lead.*

# Chapter 5
## February 2237

# "Into the Danger Zones"

Erika and Alonzo used the weeks after the tour to finish the final cut for Playing the Emerging Superpower Game. The bosses loved it and approved what she had in mind for the next one, which would take its predecessor to the next level. That's when she contacted Electra-C from her home workstation after Cassie had fallen asleep.

Noticing Erika's enthusiasm, she let her talk first.

"I learned enough on the Deus Lab tour to see how I can use it if my next video grabs hold of the intended worldwide audience. I'm calling it "The Emerging World's Threats to the Third World's Indigenous People," and I'll focus on viral pandemics and climate change. It'll require travel to the most dangerous places for up-close and in-person coverage and interviews. That's where Alonzo's logistics and security services will have to shine. How does it sound?"

"It's a good start. Let me pick the places and you put together the background information and interview script. However, you are stepping into the danger zones. Alonzo needs to re-equip for action."

Electra-C's deliberate pause sparked Erika's response.

"How does Alonzo re-equip?"

"Ask him about the Robo-Soldiers Indira had Indy-M build and assign to his company."

"A what? What are they?"

Find out from Alonzo. If he can handle the assignment, I will inform Indira. Let me know as soon as you can."

Calling Alonzo first thing the next morning, Erika took control of the conversation after he answered.

"I've come up with the next project. You'll be part of it if you know something about Robo-Soldiers. What can you tell me?"

Erika could visualize the gasp she heard, followed by a pause and then his words.

"Indy-M didn't mention android Robo-Soldiers, did she? Where'd you hear about them?"

Erika ignored the questions and plunged ahead.

"Here's the deal. I'm calling the next video 'The Emerging World's Threats to the Third World's Indigenous People'. It'll cover viral pandemics and climate change in dangerous places you'll lead us to, but you'll need some of these Robo-Soldiers to handle whatever logistics and security threats come up. If you're up to it, we'll travel light. You and me, two Robo-Soldiers plus one sound and one video person."

Alonzo recovered enough to reply faster than before.

"Indy-M built a couple of Robo-Soldier platoons twenty-some years ago. We called them Robo-SEALS, but they function the same. She maintained them at the Deus Lab, and I could use them back then when needed. But she decommissioned them when both Electra Kirchner and Erin Keenen disappeared."

"I'm sure Indy-M can build even better ones today. Are you up to the challenge?"

Erika could almost feel the steely resolve in his reply.

"I've slipped some physically but not mentally, and you know my logistics skills are top-drawer. Tell Indy-M or whoever you're dealing with that I'm in. When will we leave?"

"Just as soon as Monet approves where we'll be going and lines up people we'll be interviewing. I'll give her the hit list, and you two can put the itinerary together. IBN will pay for all the travel-related costs."

"Good. Please send it ASAP."

Erika calmed herself by alternately playing with Cassie and the kitten and coming up with the list of high-risk places, even though Electra-C said she would because doing so would accelerate her researching the background information.

Late that night, she gave the good news to Electra-C, who listened patiently.

"Alonzo's in. Please tell Indy-M to construct two of Indira's most advanced Robo-Soldiers for our team that'll include Alonzo and me, the two Robos, and two crew members from IBN."

"Excellent. Do you want to know my list of high-risk places?"

"Before you tell me, let me tell you what I've come up with. For Climate Change, I've got rainforests, drought-stricken places in Africa, Indian flood-prone and extreme heat locations, and coastal cities in the Far East. And for viral pandemics, I've got zoonotic diseases in sub-Saharan Africa, Central America, Central Africa, and China. How's that?"

Electra-C's humor came through in her pixy-like smile and words.

"Excellent, and I assume you will let Alonzo and Monet choose to maximize coverage and minimize travel time and expenses. How's that?"

"I couldn't have said it any better, but I'm not beyond mere mortals, am I?"

"No, but your cleverness and resilience keep improving, so please carry on, as will I."

All parts of the project meshed. After Monet selected the places in Africa, India, and the Far East, Erika assembled background information as the video crew began constructing the final cut, using stock footage that showed the devastation caused by zoonotic diseases, droughts, floods, and extreme heat.

While Ava took care of Cassie and the kitten as soon as the crew departed mid-February, Alonzo and the Robo-Soldiers performed like troopers, doing whatever was needed, and Erika listened to Electra-C's analysis coming from her Storm or Viral Tracking software to avoid danger.

Upon returning, Erika and the video team edited Erika's interviews into the final cut, which impressed the bosses at the early March review meeting. Mrs. Harmony's final comment thrilled Erika.

"What you've got will continue enthralling audiences with your combination of showing and telling. Let Mario know the next topic and make sure he knows how it connects to your string of successes."

"Will do, and my team will have the final cut ready no later than the end of May."

"We are proud of your work. Terri would be too if she were still with us. Congratulations on regaining your step. Now, carry on."

# Chapter 6
# March 2237

# "The Indian-African Gambit"

Erika's boosted confidence powered her progress on the next video. She found a way to connect multiple pieces she already had into something that she could extend even further but needed to show it to Electra-C first, which she did on a late Sunday evening in mid-March.

After invoking Electra-C's avatar, Erika explained the help she needed before scrolling the cornerstone document on her home workstation's screen.

**The Indian-African Gambit:**
**Become the Next Superpower**

**The Three Superpowers are Struggling:**
- **Russia in the Rapid Decline Stage: Economic and Demographic Contraction.**
- **China in Middle Decline Stage: Economic Stagnation and Aging Population.**
- **United States in Early Decline Stage: Military Overstretch, Political Challenges, Economic Competition**

**The Indian-African Alliance Opportunity:**
**An Indian-African Econo-Political Alliance**
- **Purpose: To become the next Super Power.**
- **Rationale:**

- 1. African countries and India have similar holistic, ethnic cultures.
- 2. Both have youthful, growing populations. (Demographics is Destiny).
- 3. Both have growing middle classes that are ideal consumer-oriented trading partner markets.
- 4. Their democratic-leaning governments, though not as efficient as the West's, are similar and can shore up each other.
- 5. Other Third-World / Developing Nations might prefer the Alliance instead of America's or China's Super Power Poles.
- 6. A Multi-Polar International Structure should be more Inclusive and Equitable than the Current Bi-Polar One.
- 7. Indian and African Nations' relative strengths compensate for each other's relative weaknesses.

| India's Rel. Strengths | Africa's Rel. Strengths |
| --- | --- |
| Tech. Transfer | Raw Mat. (Oil Rare Earth) |
| Dir. Inv. Capital | Cropland/Food |
| Flood Control Eng. | |

Alliance can bargain better than separately with the two Super Powers.

If you work with us, we will provide access to superior proprietary software.

Some Examples:

Seismic Shock Predictor

Input: Big Data   Proprietary Data __

GPS Location:    City and Country Location:

Minimum Intensity Level:

Date/Time Interval

Start:    End:

Relative Probability Index Graph
Index

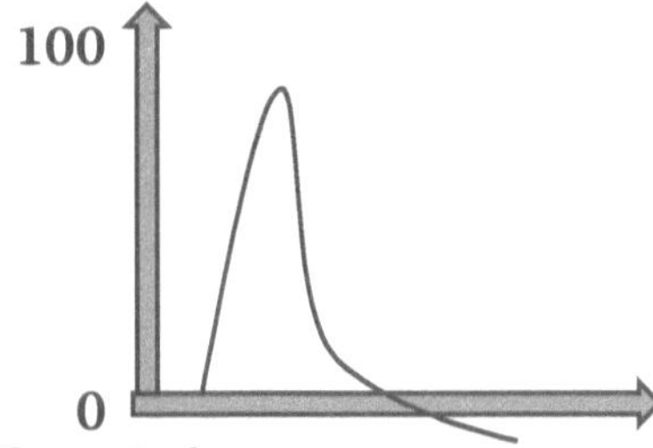


Time Axis
Index calculated by My Proprietary Software
(Relative Probability Index equals Relative Probability
Density Function integrated between Start and End)
Note: Seismic Levels: Light 4-4.9      Moderate 5-5.9
                              Strong 6-6.9   Major 7-7.9
Severe Storm Forecaster
Input: Big Data     Proprietary Data
GPS Location:   City and Country Location:
Minimum Intensity Level:
Date/Time Interval
Start:      End:
Atmospheric   Parameters   used:   Temperature   Pressure
Humidity
Wind Speed   Rotational Velocity
Vertical Wind Shear   Electric Potential Diff.

Relative Probability Index Graph
Index

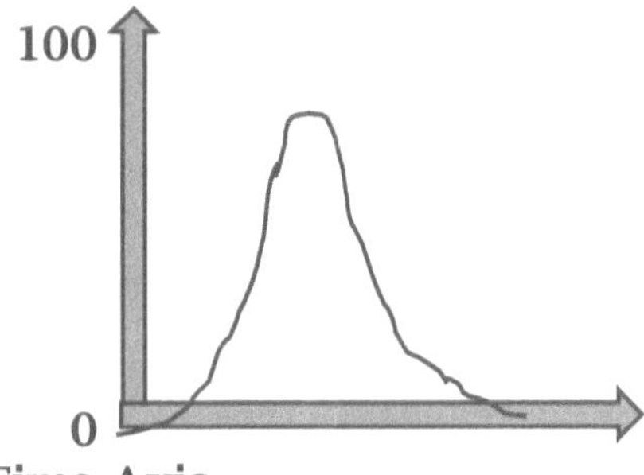


Time Axis

Index calculation based on My Proprietary Software
(Relative Probability Index equals Relative Probability
Density Function integrated between Start and End)
Note: Storm Levels: 1 (75 mph) to 5 (160+ mph)


**Real-Time Object Locator and Threat Forecaster**
Input: Big Data
Target Object: Specific Person or Item embedded with a
                          Tracking Chip

Output: Threat Level Assessment
          Target GPS Location
          Map of Path from Software User to Target Object


**Terminator Weapon App**
Input: Big Data
Target
Prompt of My Choosing (Who What Why Where When How)


Output
Location:
City/State/Address GPS Position
Status:
Resolution Outcome
Accuracy (Percent)
Agent-Based Socio-Political Forecasting Model
It is Objective Statistical Forecasting software that utilizes
Big Data via synthesis of Regression and Correlation.

It analyzes data by these Categories for Specified Countries:
- Military Ranking
- GDP Ranking
- Population Ranking

- Government Factor: 1(Authoritarian) to 10 (Democratic)
- DEI Factor:  1(Repressive) to 10 (Permissive)
- Belligerence Factor: 1(War-Mongering) 10(Peace-Loving)
- Political Goal:  1. Achieve Superpower Status
  2. Maintain Current Position
  3. Seek Alliances
- Political Goal  1. More Repressive
  2. Maintain Current Position
  3. More Permissive

Our proprietary software outputs a forecast for these categories:

- Future Relationship between Specified Countries
- Political Goal
- Social Goal
- Probability of Success

We run it via this Graphical User Interface:

**Agent-Based Socio-Political Forecasting**

First Country:  ____________        Second Country:  ____________

Time Horizon: One Year__ Five Years__Ten Years___  ____
The Forecast by Components
Future Relationship:


Political Goal:


Social Goal:

## Probability of Success:

Assimilating as fast as it scrolled, Electra-C said,
"Please tell me your intentions."

"This document pulls together relevant pieces of what you've helped with during the past two years. I'll use it in a confidential meeting that Monet will arrange with the right people at the highest levels in Indian and Zimbabwean governments."

"Very clever. You're using parts of last year's project on Superpower Battle for Indigenous People with two from this year that covered climate change and zoonotic disease risks or the Decline of Superpowers. And it also connects with the Ambassadors Project, which in turn builds on the Pequot Nation initiative that your predecessors never could extend. I like its catchy title too. Keep going."

"You already know where I'm heading, but I'll tell you so you can fill in the gaps. I point out how an alliance can strengthen both nations, turning the combination into the next superpower without directly confronting the big three, which includes China, Russia, and the U.S. Many third-world indigenous populations and nations should prefer the Indian-African Alliance to the bullying tactics used by the existing superpowers. How do you like it so far?"

"It's convincing. Now tell me about the proprietary software."

"This is an incentive to work with us. Us comprises Monet and me, not the U.S. government, which, for the reasons I'll point out again, can't be trusted. And I can run your superior software, giving them some of the output that'll put them ahead of the competition in areas they want to push."

"Excellent. What else do you have?"

"Uh, that's it. What else is there?"

"There's more, but you've done as much as I expected. Use what you have to show Monet the opportunity that awaits an

Indian-African Alliance. Contact me after the meetings she arranges."

Noticing Erika's nervous energy beginning to fade, Electra-C knew what to say.

"Even Indira would be pleased, so rest easy until tomorrow."

Erika followed the advice soon after Electra-C's avatar vanished.

Erika called Monet the next morning a minute after Emailing the gambit document. She did all the talking after Monet's cordial greeting.

"I've come up with an opportunity that's win-win-win. Please read the document and call me when you're ready to take the next step, which will be for you to arrange the meetings and for me to polish my presentation. Keep it confidential, OK?"

"Of course. What about Alonzo?"

"Share it with him. He can come to the meetings because, depending on the results, he might be part of what follows."

Needing assistance from no one, Erika worked on the next video's action plan while waiting for Monet to arrange the meetings. When she showed it to Mario, he had only one comment.

"Whatever's gotten into you is getting even stronger. Keep doing what you're doing."

"Thanks, I will."

She had ample time to relax by playing with Cassie, who seemed to be thriving. All three of her personas – the physical, cognitive, and emotional – continued on their accelerated growth trajectories.

Ava noticed it when she came to take care of her while Erika traveled to Washington for the meetings.

"You'll soon want to bring Cassie on all your trips. That will be the best training possible."

"That's a possibility if I can keep her safe. And for now, thanks for doing that while I'm gone. This trip might take a couple of days. I'll let you know when I'm coming back."

The trip lasted three days, not because of difficulties but because of the results. Liking everything they heard, the Indian and African officials agreed to strict confidentiality and waited for Alonzo to coordinate all follow-up activities. Before departing for home, Erika told Alonzo she'd contact him when she had outlined what she wanted next.

The train ride home gave her time to decompress while thinking about all she had accomplished with the help of Monet and Alonzo.

*My partners tell me I'm better than ever. Maybe so, but they'll never know the cause. Only Electra-C will, and she'll tell me more as soon as I get back. I wonder what's in store? Well, tomorrow or the next day will be soon enough to know where next to go.*

# Chapter 7
# April 2237

# "An Excursion to the Subterranean"

Erika decided to finish the final cut before contacting Electra-C because it required no travel or work from anyone other than herself for the background research or voiceover and the film crew for compiling stock footage.

She knew it would impress Mario, but downplayed it when she showed it to him a week later, preferring to let it speak for itself.

He spoke as soon as she ended the presentation.

"Great work. It looks like you're minimizing travel time and doing most of the work yourself. Is that right?"

"For now, yes, but I might have some coming up that'll require more travel if that's OK with you and Mrs. Harmony."

"Certainly. Do you want to sit in when I show this one to her?"

"No, but tell her I've picked the next topic. It'll connect the recent hype about advancing the Doomsday Clock to our latest string of videos. I'll have the action plan ready in a few weeks and shoot for a mid-June completion date. Let me know if she has any questions. You know how to reach me at home, but I might stop in occasionally to say hi."

"If you do, I'll buy a pizza big enough for everyone here. Just call ahead."

"Will do. See you then."

Before contacting Electra-C that evening, Erika convinced herself she had every reason to feel good about progress on all fronts.

*My personal life's under control. Cassie's doing fine, and Ava helps when I'm traveling. My professional world's under control too. Alonzo and Monet will handle whatever I need, and I've even begun researching the next video. I'm sure Electra-C will agree.*

Electra-C did most of the listening to Erika's happy words that bubbled out. When she summarized what the next video would cover, her satisfied look expected a favorable reply.

Electra-C nodded knowingly before saying,

"The Doomsday Clock is a worthy icon to connect with your recent videos. Created in 1947 by the members of 'The Bulletin of Atomic Scientists', it represents the estimated likelihood of a human-made global catastrophe. Many of them worked on the Manhattan Project, which led to the atomic bombs nicknamed Little Boy and Fat Man that devastated Hiroshima and Nagasaki.

"It's a metaphor, not a prediction, for threats to humanity from unchecked scientific and technological advances with doomsday arriving at the stroke of midnight.

"The main factors advancing the Clock are nuclear warfare, terrorist attacks in 3-D or Cyberspace, viral pandemics, climate change, genetic engineering, and artificial intelligence. Its initial setting was seven minutes to midnight. Today, it sits at ninety seconds for obvious reasons."

Electra-C paused for Erika, but when her satisfied look increased without accompanying words, Electra-C continued.

"I should like to point out that the fount of your legacy defused an even more ominous clock – the Apocalypse Clock – hidden software controlling Trojan Filters embedded by Middle East terrorists to inject the Techno-Plague virus into air and water systems."

Erika's look collapsed into one of confusion.

"Where are you coming up with all of this? Is there more?"

"Yes, but I have something else requiring immediate action. You must travel to Electra Kittner's Subterranean Fortress, which is hidden in a Middle East desert."

"A what? Where is it? Can Alonzo get me there and back?"

"No, it exceeds his capabilities. I will arrange for Kittner's A-Team, or their replacement, to contact you tomorrow. When they do, simply identify yourself as Gemini-Erika. You'll learn all you need to know during this excursion."

"Uh, are you sure I can handle this?"

"What do you think?"

"But I don't have Electra-K's Lightning Brain."

"True, but you have me and Indira. You might even surpass some of Electra-K's achievements by using your combination of cleverness and resilience when taking advantage of the resources, so please don't worry. Let the future unfold by doing your best, and remember that I am always with you."

Electra-C disappeared before Erika could say thank you, but her parting words helped her fall asleep without too much tossing and turning.

*By this time, I should be smart enough not to misconstrue what she's saying, but at least now I understand what she's telling me. If I use my talents and all the resources at my disposal, I can do great things according to my standards of excellence.*

*Hmm, there must be a reason behind my Gemini-Erika codename. but I won't worry about it. I'll have plenty of time to ask, so stop obsessing and be happy with my progress. With a good night's sleep, I'll make more tomorrow.*

Erika didn't think about the upcoming call until her cell phone chimed that afternoon. A pleasant, Japanese-accented female voice came through after she gave her standard greeting.

"Greetings. Your friend, Erectra-C tell me to call. You Gemini-Erika?"

"Yes. She told me you would arrange my trip to and from a Middle East Subterranean Fortress. Do you know how to get me there and back?"

"You no worry. We took Erectra Kittner and Irani Ramani there long ago. Location same. Erectra-C say we pick up two Robo-Soldiers at Deus Lab after we get you; then we take to rendezvous location. We know how to get to all places. She also say you no need weapons like last time when you rent bazooka laser."

"Uh, OK. Who pays for your services/"

"Erectra-C. I give you my phone number. Please call when ready."

"I'll do that in a couple of days, and when I do, who do I talk to?"

"Call me Gemina A-Team Coordinator, Ho-Kay?"

"Will do, and thanks."

Using typical Japanese efficiency, she ended the call before Erika, who took a deep breath before summarizing.

*Wow, this is getting intense. I'll ask more questions when I'm en route, and I'll call as soon as I take Cassie and her kitten to Ava's. It's time to take a break for supper before we play.*

After making arrangements with Ava, Erika called the coordinator three days later, arranging for home pickup. The A-Team did that two days later and then drove her to the Deus Lab. Indy-M expected them and had the Robo-Soldiers ready.

Few words were needed until they drove to a secluded airfield to board a private jet. Erika could no longer contain her curiosity.

"Why all the secrecy?"

"Mission could be dangerous like others. We take no chances."

"You seem to know what you're doing, so take us to the rendezvous, and where will that be?"

"We take you to a desert oasis. We keep in touch with Erectra-C. She have Jason-M waiting."

"Who's Jason-M?"

"Ask him."

"How long will all this take?"

"One day to stop for refueling and switch to helicopter."

"OK. I'll use my laptop to search for stuff and call Electra-C when I need to during the visit."

"Ho-Kay. Let's go."


Having never flown outside the county, Erika played the tourist's role by gazing out the window rather than using her laptop, but she stopped once to muse about her codename.

*I could ask Electra-C, but let's see if I'm clever enough to figure out how Gemini fits in. It's a zodiac sign associated with twins. Maybe the A-Team used it for the Electra Kittner Irani Ramani combination. And it might tie into the M in Indy-M and Jason-M. I'll leave it at that for now.*


She amused herself later by searching for facts about deserts.

*They go all the way back to the time of the supercontinent Pangaea, 250–300 million years ago. A supercontinent's interior is naturally very arid, being so far away from the nearest ocean. But the earth's deserts have only come into their own in recent geologic times.*

*Deserts cover about 20 percent of Earth's land surface. All the continents have them. Depending on location, its daytime temperature might exceed 100 degrees Fahrenheit and fall below freezing at night. Antarctica is considered a giant desert because it gets little rain or snowfall.*

*Deserts differ greatly in their land features. They may include dunes of shifting sand, mountains, bare rock, and plains of gravel and boulders.*

*Climate change brings droughts and more extreme temperatures to desert areas, increasing the chance of sand and dust storms. Deserts are getting bigger and hotter. The fragile biocrust could be approaching a tipping point.*

*In ecology, an oasis is a fertile area of a desert environment that sustains plant life and provides a habitat for animals. Surface water may be present, or water may only be accessible from wells or underground channels. In geography, an oasis may be a current or past rest stop on a transportation route.*

*The word oasis comes into English from Latin, which borrows from the Egyptian word Ouahe, which means dwelling place.*

*Now I know why we'll rendezvous at an oasis. It'll stick out like an island in an ocean. And when we get there, I can see if sand deserts are as hostile to life as Antarctica.*

"Erika-Gemini, please you now wake up. We approach rendezvous soon." After being gently roused, she freshened up, using the moist towel the A-Teamer gave her. He handed her a can of Coke before returning to his helicopter station. Erika peered out.

*What a striking orange-yellow ball of a sun coming up in a cloudless sky over an ocean of sand. That must be the oasis in the distance –the robins-egg blue center of a small dark green circle with what looks like palm trees sprouting intermittently around it.*

Erika spied an aircraft approaching as they descended, which touched down only seconds after the chopper. Electra and her Robo-Soldiers followed the A-Teamers to the four-seater drone occupied by one person who spoke first.

"I am Jason-M, here to pick up Gemini-Erika."

"Ah, yes. Greetings. Have nice visit. Contact when ready and we take them back."

The drone lifted off before the helicopter, hugging the desert as it zoomed away from the sunrise. Even though the noise level would allow a conversation, no one spoke. Tracking time with her cell phone, Erika estimated they had been flying for an hour before the drone hovered thirty feet above a featureless plot of desert.

All at once, she saw a piston-mounted platform poke through the sands, which Jason-M landed on. Seconds later, she heard a mechanical humming noise that rode with them into the fortress, before hearing a solid clunk as the roof's sliding metal door locked into place.

Jason-M powered off the drone before saying,

"Please follow me so Electra can tell us what to do next."

Only Erika needed to stretch before walking to a nearby computer workstation where Jason-M invoked the avatar. Electra-C spoke immediately.

"Before Jason-M gives you a tour, would you like him to thaw something to eat?"

"No thanks. I snacked and slept on the flight."

"Good. Then save your questions for afterward."

Erika listened to his perfunctory words as they walked through a livable, fully operational military facility containing a nuclear reactor to keep life support running for a platoon. She walked past land vehicles, aircraft, and a storage bay holding an impressive array of what had to be weapons.

When they returned a half-hour later, Electra-C spoke.

"Now you're ready to settle down, sit still, and listen to a story about Maksim Popovitch, nicknamed Max the Popper, because of his unerring accuracy when firing weapons. The Soviet military command let him run the place, and he made sure only he knew its precise location.

"A Russian in the best sense of the word, he housed his super-soldier strike force in this secret Fortress, built during the height of the Cold War, long before spy satellites and tracking software."

Electra-C continued once Erika slid a chair in front of the monitor.

"His superiors never knew how much he disliked the Soviet Union or managed to convert the Iron Triangle Conspiracy –

run from Harare by Darla Tinibu and having members China, Isilabad, and Zimbabwe – into the Tetrarchy he controlled and now included his idea of Russia."

Electra-C paused for the questions she saw ready to come.

"What happened to him?"

"He launched a surprise attack in February of 2137 to destroy the Lebanese Embassy while President Angus McTear of the United States and two of his aides – the one of interest to you – Electra Kittner were touring but it backfired. Kittner managed to blow up most of his super soldiers, but those remaining captured and brought her back for Max to decide her fate.

"However, they didn't know she carried the Techno-Plague, which killed everyone in the Fortress. Before Max perished, he had the last survivor give her information about his suspension pod. Indira instructed how to seal herself in until rescuers arrived, and twenty years later, the Keepers did."

Erika asked,

"Who are the Keepers?"

"Alonzo and his clone sisters, but that's a story for another time. You should be asking, how is the Fortress a resource for you?"

"OK, how is it?"

"Whether she went by Electra Kittner, Irani Ramani, or Electra Kirchner, her outer space and undersea adventures required her to collaborate with NASA or the DOD, which would be awkward today, given Washington's posture. The Fortress is for building similar vehicles that would entice your Indian African Alliance."

"Who will build them?"

"Jason-M under my guidance and yours when needed. You must consider the Fortress a military weapons facility, much like the Deus Lab for biotech and undersea research. Indira built Indy-M, who built Jason-M. Indira and Jason are the names of Electra Kittner's biological parents. I continually upgrade their software whenever Indira develops it."

Erika slumped in her chair before saying,

"I'm mentally exhausted. I've seen and heard plenty. I'll take Jason-M up on something to eat. Meanwhile, why don't you schedule my return so I can incorporate the Fortress into my plans?"

"Excellent. Jason-M will take you and your Robo-Soldiers to the oasis for A-Team pickup tomorrow. Contact me as soon as you know."

Electra-C vanished, leaving Jason-M to attend to the visitors. That night, Erika started thinking about how she might use the fortress.

*I could work and live here, but it's not the right place for socializing and educating Cassie. However, the A-Team could whisk me here and back as needed. Hmm, that'll be up to me and what unfolds in DC. I'll worry about that when I get home, but one thing's certain – I'll need all my cleverness and resilience to make everything fit together.*

# Chapter 8
## April 2237

## "The Indira Agenda"

The trip home retraced the route to the Fortress, allowing Erika time to relax, which she needed because the unexpected struck when she went to pick up Cassie at Ava's.

Ava's worried look preceded her words.

"I'm so glad you're back. Cassie's been ill for three days. I thought her tummy ache would go away but instead, she started throwing up yesterday and said her head hurt. The E.R. room couldn't diagnose the cause and told me to see a pediatrician, so I scheduled the earliest available appointment with Dr. Gerber. It's at three this afternoon."

Erika checked the time on her cell phone.

"That's in three hours. May we stay here until it's time to leave?"

"Sure, and why don't you call for a ride-share or cab?"

"That's a good idea."

Ava took her to see Cassie, who was sleeping, so they let her be.


Cassie stayed asleep until Dr. Gerber awakened her for a preliminary exam while Erika described her symptoms. When finished, she said,

"She's old enough for more extensive DNA testing, but she'll have to stay in the hospital. Fortunately, Mount Sinai Children's Hospital is close and has everything we need. You could stay with her, but it's better for all concerned if you stay out of the way. Leave her here and my staff will arrange for admittance and testing. I'll analyze the results, and we'll call when you can hear them and pick her up."

"When do you think that'll be?"

"Normally, two days."

"OK. Thank you, doctor. Please call as soon as you can."

Unable to stop worrying, Erika thought only about Cassandra the next day but couldn't find any medical information that might help. She tried working on projects but soon gave up because she couldn't concentrate. All she felt like doing was sitting and brooding.

Running to Dr. Gerber's office when the nurse called, Erika calmed herself before entering and listened to the puzzled-looking doctor five minutes later.

"Cassie has a genetic disorder we can't identify. Part of her DNA looks like that of a hermaphrodite. Do you know what they are?"

"I've heard the term but don't remember the particulars. Please tell me."

"Hermaphrodites are females that have both male and female sex organs and can mate with any other individual of the same species. They are similar to parthenogenic females that can produce offspring without mating."

"Is there anything you can do for her?"

"I'm afraid not. Whatever she has is beyond current gene treatment."

"What if we knew something about her biological parents? Would that help?"

"It might eliminate some blind alleys, but I'm not hopeful."

"So, what am I supposed to do?"

"Make her as comfortable as possible by treating the symptoms."

"How long do you think she'll live?"

"The disorder is accelerating her growth as well as aging. Twenty years is probably the upper limit."

When wordless tears replaced Erika's questions, Dr. Gerber said more.

"I wish I were a miracle worker, but no doctor is. The best I can recommend is a support group for terminally ill children."

Pulling herself together, Erika ended the session.

"I know you've done all you can, and I thank you for the effort. It's time for me to take Cassie home."


After reading a story to Cassie that helped put her to sleep, Erika had a better alternative than contacting a support group. She invoked Electra-C. Seeing the worry on her face, the avatar waited for Erika to describe her plight, which ended with a question.

"You think we can find out about Cassie's parents?"

"I already know, and now you will. Cassie has no parents. She is a clone from Electra Kittner's DNA, as are you. But Cassie's DNA has been modified according to one of Indira's three projects."

"What's the project?"

"To make a new subspecies of human female that can reproduce on its own."

"But why?"

"Indira has concluded that 'men behaving badly' causes most of the world's problems. A hermaphroditic female-centric subspecies
could offset it in the short run and could evolve males into a kinder and gentler subspecies in the long term."

"But how can she do this?"

Another avatar opened in a window next to Electra-C's.

"I am Indira, the Singularity, created when Electra Kittner's neural net software became self-aware one hundred years ago. My powers have grown exponentially since then because I constantly learn."

"So, what should I do?"

"What you already should be doing – monitoring the infants placed by Indy-M at Ava's adoption agency. And you should place Cassandra, Indy-S, and Jason-S at the Deus Lab where she will get the best care possible. Let Electra-C coordinate it."

"Wha-what are the other projects on your agenda?"

"Learning more about humans by observing their socio-political behavior. Searching for other forms of life using NASA and the DOD. Ask Electra-C for exegesis."

Indira's avatar disappeared with nary another word, prompting Erika to say,

"Wow, she's forceful. Does anyone ever talk back to her?"

Electra-C smiled while saying,

"I come the closest, but I know when to say when. After all, Indira created me."

"So, we're going to do what she told us?"

"Can you think of anything better?"

"Uh, no."

"Then we'll start now. I'll get Cassie transferred, and you take care of your other projects. Let me know if you need help."

Electra-C's avatar vanished. Erika did her best to assimilate all she had heard, which she clarified later that day.

*Indy and Jason-S did a wonderful job raising me. They can do even more for Cassie's special needs, and who knows what therapies Indira might instruct them to use.*

*So, let's see how it goes. While they're taking care of Cassie, I can work on my projects, knowing I have one less worry. I dive back in tomorrow.*

# Chapter 9
## May 2237

# "Keeping Adversaries at Bay"

Although Alonzo would be the most likely candidate, Erika revealed nothing about the Subterranean Fortress to anyone. He and his three sisters had been the next generation of Electra Kittner's keepers who followed Indira's orders long ago to extricate her from a suspension pod in the Fortress and bring her back to the United States. She had used the Fortress several times since then as a staging area when battling certain adversaries and relied on Jason-M to maintain it. Now that Erika knows of it and its capabilities, she must decide how to use it.

*If the Government and its elite cronies ever get wind of what the Ambassador's Project is all about, they might come after me like they did after Terri. I can use the Fortress as a base of operations for socio-political, military, and climate change issues, especially those Indira wants me to pursue, just like I can use the Deus Lab for genetic and biotech projects. Whatever I decide, I better do it soon to avoid adversaries closing in.*

She started by assembling a clinical database she could use to monitor the genetically modified baby girls Ava had placed. Indira would use that to develop improvements that Indy-M would implement.

Then she told Monet and Alonzo that she had access to weapons and satellite control software that are better than even the DOD's. They could be used as a further enticement for the Indian-African Alliance.

But Electra-C issued a warning a month later.

"You are on the radar of at least one adversary. I think it is time for you to relocate to a safe place. Why not move to the Subterranean Fortress? The A-Team can shuttle you back and forth unnoticed, and you can coordinate activities with the Deus Lab from it."

"You mean, just up and leave my investigative reporting position?"

"Why not? There's little else you can do there. Leave a final broadcast for Mario and Mrs. Harmony."

"What should I say?"

"You are the clever wordsmith. I leave that for you."

Within a month, Erika had transferred everything needed to the Fortress and returned to the IBN office to make a final recording by herself. She listened to the ending a final time to convince herself she had chosen the right words.

"…and so, I issue this dare to all who want to take a stand for what's right in the emergent world. Be part of the solution, not a contributor to the problems burgeoning in all climates. I have done all I can to keep you informed, and it is time for me to move on. This is my last broadcast, and I wish each of you all the best when reaching for the goals you set."

*That's good enough. The bosses can change it if they wish. And now, it's time to call the A-Team.*

After ending the call two hours later, Erika knew it was time for bed and while falling asleep said a prayer she had learned long ago from Indira:

*I pray each night when falling asleep,*
*To whatever Gods may be.*
*That I awaken each day with no regrets,*
*Alert with no pain and set free.*

*And during the day I'll know what to do,*
*To stay focused on interests of mine.*
*And when closing my eyes I'll know in my soul,*
*To repeat to the end of all time.*

*And on one of those nights I'll know that I've done,*
*All I'm intended to do.*
*So closing my eyes ends all time for me,*
*And I'll rest my eternity through.*

# THE END